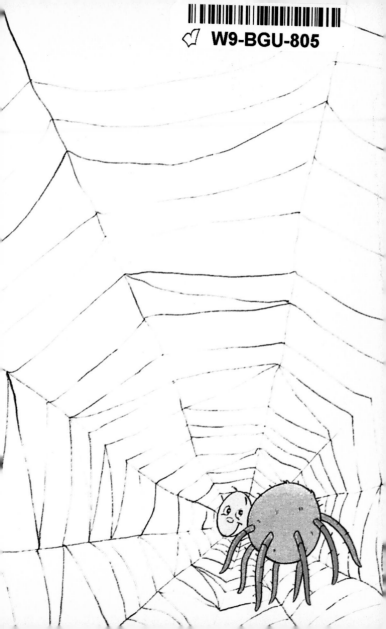

© 1994 Geddes & Grosset Ltd
Published by Geddes & Grosset Ltd,
New Lanark, Scotland.

ISBN 1 85534 577 3

Printed and bound in Slovenia.

The Town Mouse and the Country Mouse

Retold by Judy Hamilton
Illustrated by R. James Binnie

Tarantula Books

There was once a small brown mouse who lived in a little nest at the edge of a field, deep in the countryside. Life in the country was not easy and he had to work hard to find food, but he was perfectly content. He had many good friends, his nest was cosy and comfortable and after a hard day's work, he always slept well and woke refreshed, to the sounds of nature.

One day, the country mouse arrived home after gathering food for the winter and found a letter waiting for him, from his cousin the town mouse.

"I am coming to visit you next week," it said. "I am looking forward to seeing you and learning about the countryside."

The country mouse was delighted at the thought of meeting his cousin. He set to work at once, gathering extra food and making up another cosy little bed with fresh straw and leaves. He told all his friends about his visitor.

At last the day of the town mouse's arrival dawned, and the country mouse was up bright and early. He set out a feast of grains and berries that he had in his foodstore. He waited all day, but when it began to get dark and there was still no sign of the town mouse, the country mouse was getting very worried. At last, a bedraggled, dirty, grey figure staggered up the lane towards the country mouse's nest.

The country mouse hugged his cousin with relief.

"Whatever happened to you?" he asked. The town mouse's fur was damp and muddy, and his nose was scratched.

"It was terrible!" exclaimed the town mouse. "I was walking across this horrible muddy field on my way here, and a geat big bird suddenly dived down towards me. I was trying to run away when I tripped and fell in a patch of particularly sticky mud. I managed to get up again, but the bird was still after me. I ran as fast as I could to the edge of the field, where I saw a hole in the ground and I dived straight into it and bashed my poor nose!"

He rubbed his nose gingerly, still trembling with fright after his ordeal. He really was a sorry sight.

"Have some supper," said the country mouse kindly. "I should have warned you to keep well hidden from hawks and owls. You must always be on your guard."

The town mouse looked suspiciously at the grain and berries laid out for him.

"Is this all you have to eat?" he asked. Then he realised he was being rather rude and added, "It's just that in the town there are so many tasty foods, like bread and cheese, sugary cakes and the most delicious pastries!"

The country mouse had never heard of such things.

"I quite like the food that I can get around here," he said, "And I am sure you will like it too. The country air will give you quite an appetite!"

But the town mouse did not enjoy his supper, and the country air was cold! He decided that it was time to snuggle up in bed for the night.

"I'm rather tired," he said to the country mouse. "Could you please show me where I am to sleep?"

So the country mouse proudly showed his cousin the fresh straw bed which he had made for him. The town mouse tried to make himself comfortable, but the straw was very scratchy. It was not at all what he was used to. He tossed and turned all night until morning came. The country mouse came to find him bleary-eyed and grumpy.

"You need fresh air!" said the country mouse. "Come and help me to gather winter stores!"

The country mouse set off into the woods with his cousin trailing reluctantly behind him. The town mouse did not like working, especially when it was so dirty and damp. The country mouse set to work gathering berries and nuts from the forest floor.

"Why do you have to get so much food now for the winter?" asked the town mouse.

"Food is scarce in the winter," replied his cousin. "We have to store things up now while supplies are plentiful or we may not have enough for the cold weather."

The town mouse was surprised. In town, there was plenty food all year round.

They finished working in the woods and the country mouse led the way towards the wheat field.

The town mouse puffed and panted as he tried to keep up. The path to the wheat field lay across a field where some cows grazed. The ground was very rough and the town mouse was watching his feet in case he tripped, so he did not notice the cows at first. Then all of a sudden he heard a loud "MOO!" behind him. He yelled and jumped high in the air. The country mouse laughed at him.

"Don't worry, it's only a cow!" he said.

But the town mouse was NOT amused.

"I have had quite enough of life in the country," he announced. "If you ask me, it's cold, dirty and dangerous! AND the food is awful! I'm going back to town and I'm going to take you with me, cousin, to show you what a good life is really like!"

That evening, the country mouse found himself on a train with his cousin, heading towards the town. The train was very noisy and smelly but the country mouse was excited about his visit. However, when the two mice scrambled off the train at the station, the country mouse was in for a shock. The train had been noisy, but the bustle and roar of the station was much worse! When the town mouse led the way out into the street, the country mouse was terrified by the crowds of people hurrying by, and the rattling and roaring of the cars and lorries and the screeching of brakes. The country mouse thought that he would choke on the exhaust fumes!

"Oh!" gasped the country mouse to his cousin, "Take me to your nest, quickly, please!"

The town mouse laughed.

"You'll get used to it!" he said cheerfully as he guided the country mouse through the tramping feet towards a huge, grey building along the street. "Lucky for you that I live close to the station!" and he dived down a grating at the side of the building.

The country mouse followed close behind as the town mouse found his way along dark, underground tunnels and then climbed upwards towards a hole, high in the wall. When they came out at the other side of the hole, they were on a shelf in a cool, dark room full of food.

"Here we are!" beamed the town mouse. "This is the pantry. There's no need to go gathering wheat here! – Tuck in!"

The country mouse had never seen so much food. He darted everywhere, tasting everything. He was amazed to find four kinds of cheese and ate heartily from each one. He was just finishing with a large chunk of fruit cake when he caught sight of a big, black, furry shadow on the wall, and heard an ominous hissing noise. His cousin suddenly pushed him hard.

"Quick! Run for it! That's the cat!" he cried.

The country mouse made for the hole as fast as he could, just as the cat pounced. The country mouse dived into the hole, struggling free just as the cat clawed his tail.

"Oh, please let's go to bed!" he gasped, wincing from the throbbing in his poor tail.

The country mouse's bed was made of feathers and scraps of material. It was tucked in behind the skirting board in one of the rooms of the house and was soft and warm, but the feathers tickled the country mouse's nose. He had eaten too much rich food and his stomach was churning. And his poor tail was sore! Poor country mouse couldn't sleep! He was woken from a restless doze by a strange humming noise outside the skirting board. He pushed his nose out of the nearest mousehole to see, but the town mouse hauled him back. The country mouse gasped as the silver nose of the vacuum cleaner whizzed past, sucking up everything in its path with a fearful "Whoosh!"

"I can't stand this any more!" wailed coumtry mouse. "I have to get back to the country!"

The town mouse kindly saw his cousin onto the train. The two mice hugged each other.

"I suppose that we are both too used to our own way of life," said the town mouse, "but at least we have lots to tell our friends about!"

The country mouse smiled. They certainly had!

It was late when the country mouse arrived back at his nest. He sighed as he took in the familiar surroundings. It was good to be home! The past few days had been exciting for both mice, but neither of them would ever want to swap places.

"I like my life just the way it is!" the country mouse smiled to himself, as he snuggled down in his own little straw bed with a contented little yawn.

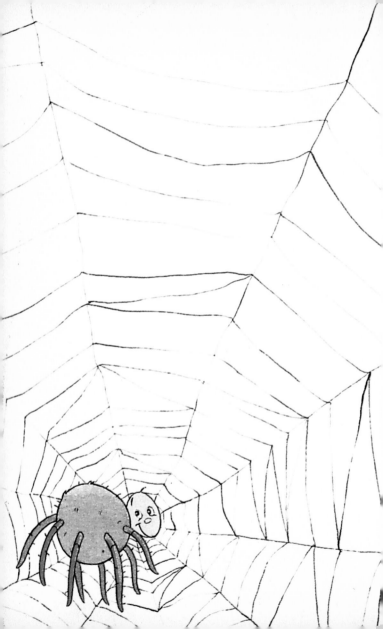